# 詩眠集

羅拔雙語詩集

# 台灣詩學吹鼓吹詩人叢書出版緣起

蘇紹連

「台灣詩學季刊雜誌社」創辦於一九九二年十二月六日，這是台灣詩壇上一個歷史性的日子，這個日子開啟了台灣詩學時代的來臨。《台灣詩學季刊》在前後任社長向明和李瑞騰的帶領下，經歷了兩位主編白靈、蕭蕭，至二○○二年改版為《台灣詩學學刊》，由鄭慧如主編，以學術論文為主，附刊詩作。二○○三年六月十一日設立「吹鼓吹詩論壇」網站，從此，一個大型的詩論壇終於在台灣誕生了。二○○五年九月增加《台灣詩學·吹鼓吹詩論壇》刊物，由蘇紹連主編。《台灣詩學》以雙刊物形態創詩壇之舉，同時出版學術面的評論詩學，及以詩創作為主的刊物。

「吹鼓吹詩論壇」網站定位為新世代新勢力的網路詩社群，並以「詩腸鼓吹，吹響詩號，鼓動詩潮」十二字為論壇主旨，典出自於唐朝·馮贄《雲仙雜記·二、俗耳針砭，詩腸鼓吹》：「戴顒春日攜雙柑斗酒，人問何之，曰：『往聽黃鸝聲，此俗耳針砭，詩腸鼓吹，汝知之乎？』」因黃鸝之聲悅耳動聽，可以發人清思，激發詩興，詩興的激發必須砭去俗思，代以雅興。論壇的名稱「吹鼓吹」三字響亮，而且論壇主旨旗幟鮮明，立即驚動了網路詩界。

「吹鼓吹詩論壇」網站在台灣網路執詩界牛耳是不爭的事實，詩的創作者或讀者們競相加入論壇為會員，除於論壇發表詩作、賞評回覆外，更有擔任版主者參與論壇版務的工作，一起推動論壇的輪子，繼續邁向更為寬廣的網路詩創作及交流場域。在這之中，有許多潛質優異的詩人逐漸浮現出來，他們的詩作散發耀眼的光芒，深受詩壇前輩們的矚目，諸如鯨向海、楊佳嫻、林德俊、陳思嫻、李長青、羅浩原、然靈、阿米、陳牧宏、羅毓嘉、林禹瑄……等人，都曾是「吹鼓吹詩論壇」的版主，他們現今已是能獨當一面的新世代頂尖詩人。

　　「吹鼓吹詩論壇」網站除了提供像是詩壇的「星光大道」或「超級偶像」發表平台，讓許多新人展現詩藝外，還把優秀詩作集結為「年度論壇詩選」於平面媒體刊登，以此留下珍貴的網路詩歷史資料。二〇〇九年起，更進一步訂立「台灣詩學吹鼓吹詩人叢書」方案，鼓勵在「吹鼓吹詩論壇」創作優異的詩人，出版其個人詩集，期與「台灣詩學」的宗旨「挖深織廣，詩寫台灣經驗；剖情析采，論說現代詩學」站在同一高度，留下創作的成果。此一方案幸得「秀威資訊科技有限公司」應允，而得以實現。今後，「台灣詩學季刊雜誌社」將戮力於此項方案的進行，每半年甄選一至三位台灣最優秀的新世代詩人出版詩集，以細水長流的方式，三年、五年，甚至十年之後，這套「詩人叢書」累計無數本詩集，將是台灣詩壇在二十一世紀中一套堅強而整齊的詩人叢書，也將見證台灣詩史上這段期間新世代詩人的成長及詩風的建立。

　　若此，我們的詩壇必然能夠再創現代詩的盛唐時代！讓我們殷切期待吧。

二〇一四年一月修訂

# 【推薦序】

余學林

　　從開始寫詩至今約莫十八年，從事外語翻譯六年，現在本業是醫學研究，什麼都要沾點邊，也總是徘徊邊緣，某種程度上堪稱自得其樂的我，接獲羅拔的邀約，對我來說是抬舉，也是一項重責大任。

　　首先，我想討論「雙語詩」。

　　廣義的「雙語詩」是以不同語言版本呈現同一首詩，但假設如此，「雙語詩」和「翻譯詩」又有何差別？我認為「雙語詩」的其中一種「定義」或「種類」應是「同一作者的意識流，用兩種不同語言去詮釋」。這樣的創作方式，是否可稱為「獨立雙語詩」？兩人以上所作的稱為「偕同雙語詩」？「雙語詩」的定義，尚須時光的醞釀，於此序文，我們姑且用上述的定義吧。

　　詩的「原形」存在於思緒中，詩人「看見」了這樣的「原形」，以兩種語言作為媒介，創造出「雙語詩」。既

然是同一作者的創作，即使文本上有歧異也是可以被接受的，（雙語詩的作者就是有這樣的「主角威能」）有時候這樣的歧異是互補的。

下面舉幾個例子，來討論羅拔的雙語詩。

《Stars／星辰》一詩短短三行，但言簡意深，包含起承轉合，也呈現出雙語詩的自由度。詩中首先將情景定錨於「夜晚」，接續「雙眼閃爍」，讓我們以為自己正看著星空，然而詩人話鋒一轉，解釋我們的視線其實「在名為網頁的天空」，我們的眼睛即是星星，主客互換，張力即生。

英文內容「All the night／All our eyes shine／On the sky named website」中，可見到前兩句使用「首語重複法」（Anaphora），但中文內容「整個夜晚／我們的雙眼閃爍／在名為網頁的天空」，前兩句為求語順而放棄這樣的技法。英文後兩句使用「非全韻」（Imperfect rhyme），中文後兩句則是用「爍」與「空」這兩個不合格押韻則實音近的方式處理。

《孩子／The Child》展現出中英文之間的差異性與互補性，中文內容其中一句「怒吼酒瓶玻璃瘀青」，乍看之下是一連串的蒙太奇，但當看見英文內容的「Winebottles brokenglassbruisesscreams」，才驚覺有這樣的急躁與壓迫感。雖然中文沒有類似的呈現手法，但是一個「漢字」中所蘊含的訊息量，用很少的空間傳達出很多的意思。

「拭淚」、「什麼是家？」相較於「he wipes his tears」、「What is home to him?」而言，就顯得較為簡短，當然這也與英文文法非常需要主詞存在於一個完整的句子有關。

既然羅拔找我寫序，應該早有心理準備我會套用統計方法：

平均中文字數：64字
標準差：41字
中位數：35字
最小值：11字
最大值：294字

平均英文字數：48字
標準差：57字
中位數：46字
最小值：10字
最大值：204字

根據上述數據可以得知，羅拔偶有篇幅較長的作品，但創作的大多是短詩，易於消化，即使是忙碌的上班族亦適用。

羅拔性格溫厚而蘊藏熱情，詩風樸實卻不時地為讀者帶來驚喜，他寫生活、寫電影、寫私人情感，有時紀念家

人，有時描繪社會，作品時而溫馨，時而逗趣，時而驚悚，白天他揹著一袋玻璃瓶去採集世界各地的土壤，深夜在庭院裡栽培花草，每一瓶土壤，他會播種兩次，用不同的種子。這就是你手中的《詩眠集》。

　　詩人少，雙語詩人甚少，我們的蕞爾小島能生出幾個雙語詩人？而羅拔正是其中一個孜孜不倦的少數。十年磨一劍，即使是再溫厚的詩人，也終有出鞘的一天。如今有幸見證結束修行出關的羅拔，我與有榮焉。我相信，羅拔會繼續寫，我們也會繼續讀。

　　入口到了，歡迎光臨羅拔的詩園。

二〇一九・一・二十一　於奧克蘭

# 【 Foreword 】

Lennex Hsueh-Lin Yu

It has been around 18 years since I started writing poetry and 6 years since I started working as a translator. And my full-time job is a medical science researcher. I have experiences in many things, but never an expert in anything. I guess I am happy with that. Receiving the invitation from Rob to write the foreword for his poetry collection is a great honour and a worrying responsibility.

To start, I would like to talk about "bilingual poetry".

A broad definition of "bilingual poetry" is one single poem with two different language versions. If this definition holds true, what then are the differences between "bilingual poetry" and "translated poetry"? I think one definition or type of "bilingual poetry" may be "the flow of consciousness of a single poet interpreted in two different languages". Perhaps such creation can be called "independent bilingual poetry", whereas that is created by two or more participants may be called "accompanied bilingual poetry". A proper definition requires time to brew, and for the time being let us accept the aforementioned definition.

The "source" of poetry exists in the mind, of which the poet "sees" and uses two languages to bring forth the abstract into physical existence of "bilingual poetry". As each pair of poems is written by the same poet, even if there are differences in the poetry, they should be tolerable (due to the invincibility of authorship) and sometimes they may complement each other.

I shall use a couple of examples below to discuss Rob's bilingual poetry.

"Stars/星辰" consists of merely three lines. While simple, it bears deep meanings, contains an introduction, elucidation of the theme, transition and a conclusion, and demonstrates the freedom a bilingual poet has. In the first line, the scene is set at "night", followed by "our eyes shine", hinting as if we are looking at the starry night sky. However, the last line reveals that our eyes are shining "on the sky named website". Our eyes are in fact the stars. The change between subject and object creates tension in this poem.

In the English version, "All the night/All our eyes shine/On the sky named website", we can see the use of anaphora in the first two lines, which was abandoned by the poet in the Chinese version ("整個夜晚／我們的雙眼閃爍／在名為網頁的天空") for the sake of fluency. Imperfect rhyme was used in the second and third line of the English version, whereas in the Chinese version, non-rhyming but similar-sounding characters "爍 (shuò)" and "空 (kong)" were used to accommodate for imperfect rhyme.

"孩子/The Child" demonstrated the variability and complementarity between Chinese and English. In the Chinese version, one line wrote "怒吼酒瓶玻璃瘀青", which seems like the use of montage. It is not until we see the English version "Winebottlesbrokenglassbruisesscreams" that we realized the irritability and pressure. Although such technique cannot be applied in Chinese, the Chinese characters are complex units that contain larger amount of information in the same space used. "拭淚" and "什麼是家？" seem more compact than "he wipes his tears" and "What is home to him?" respectively. Of course, it also has to do with the necessity of a subject in a complete sentence in English grammar.

Since Rob asked me to write the foreword for him, then surely, he had prepared to see some statistics on his poetry collection.

<u>Chinese characters</u>

Mean:64

Standard deviation: 41

Median: 35

Minimum: 11

Maximum: 294

<u>English words</u>

Mean: 48

Standard deviation: 57

Median: 46

Minimum: 10

Maximum: 204

Based on the statistics, it is known that occasionally Rob writes longer poems, but the vast majority of his work are short poems, easily digestible even for busy white-collars.

Rob is a gentleman with immanent passion. His poems are simple yet sometimes bring you surprises. He writes about life, movies, personal feelings. Sometimes he commemorates his family members and sometimes he depicts the society. His poems are sometimes heart-warming, sometimes funny, and sometimes, straight-up horrifying. During the day, he carries a bag of glass bottles to collect different kinds of soils from all around the world. At night he plants different seeds twice in each kind of soil. And that is the poetry collection you are holding.

There are few poets in this world, let alone bilingual poets. How many will there be in Taiwan? Well, Rob is one of the dedicated few. It is said in Chinese "ten years to make a sword". This day would come eventually, even for the humblest poet. I have been honoured to witness Rob's epiphany. I believe Rob will keep on writing, and we will keep on reading.

Here we are at the entrance. Welcome to Rob's garden of poetry.

21$^{st}$ January 2019 in Auckland

# 【推薦序】

袁鶴翔

「音」和「形」是中文的兩大構成要素，故王筠在《文字蒙求》一文中提出這兩點，認為幼兒識字須由此兩點開始。「形」指「意象」，「音」指「發聲」亦是聲音。在辭的創作方面，二者是不可缺一的，儘管在現代詩中，我們似乎對音節的重視不太在意，可是讀詩時總希望能朗朗上口，在音韻方面能夠「誦」。當然有時亦可用「意象」來代替「音韻」，近代詩即是如此，但詩的節奏仍是需要顧到。故而近代口語（白話）詩，特別注重「意象」。「意象」的巧妙運用，更是作詩者用心、用力所在之處。它一方面從簡單的「指事」，領讀者會意詩的所言，進入詩的主旨。另一方面，亦誘讀者由此產生心靈上的迴響，這是詩人從文字構成「意象」（IMAGE），引起讀者「心生共鳴」的主要原因。正立的詩做到了。

正立的詩集共分兩大部，一為「無眠大地」，第二部是「無夢天堂」，第一部分主題是人生經驗的抽象化，有主觀經驗的客觀呈現，如〈小妹離家〉一詩中的表述，亦有現代詩中著重純「意象」的描述，如〈鴉〉這首詩即是。後者令人憶起休姆（Hulme）的〈泊橋上〉（Above the Dock）一詩中，對「意象」的著筆。第二部分是從現實描寫中，投射到意識思維的抽象世界，有個人的經歷、想像、思考，亦有更深入的意識抽象化的表達，如〈中年〉一首即是。可是一、二這部又不是那麼經緯分明；二者是相互交替地呈現出個人心靈的感受和客觀世界，雖「分」而又「合」的一種境界，既是主觀的，又是客觀的詩的創作和描述。這是難得的成就，這是詩。

　　正立的詩集是集合經驗和抽象思考的一種創意的表現。希望他能在這一基礎上，更上一層樓，我拭目以待。

二〇一九・二月　於高雄

# 【Foreword】

YUAN, Heh-Hsiang

Words create two most enduring impressions in our mind and make us stretch our imagination to an immense vision which embraces both reality and beyond.

Nothing can catch for us this ingenious combination of the world outside of us and that inside us. Poetry is one measure that enables us to experience such wonder.

For those who write poetry, word means sound and image. Sound gives us the musicality of language, and word the shape of things. Often, the two combine to give us, the reader, a sharpened sense of sound and sight; they echo the throe of our feelings and quicken the pace of our mental pulse. Rob's poems give us just that, the world within and the world without; yet, the two are intricately and delicately balanced. In part one, "Land without Sleep", we feel the personal through a recollection of parting emotions between the loved ones. There is a sense of sorrow as a brother parts with a sister, a lover with a love, youthful innocence with aging experience. Life is a journey from one end to the other. In part two, "Heaven without Dream", the theme embraces more; there is hope unfulfilled or dreams unrealized.

The tone varies with the theme of each poem, thus variability becomes tuneful changes as the poetic motif develops with each poem.

In modern poetry, the attention catcher is not sound but image. If we accept the revolutionary turn in modern poetry by citing Hulme's "Above the Dock", we find in Rob's work, "Crows", a familiar emphasis. "A thousand dark refugees/ Howling, crushing the setting sun" remind us just a similar imagistic vividness. That is poetry also. The two, sentiment and image, are both found in Rob's collection of poems.

As a young poet, this is quite an achievement. I congratulate Rob on his good work and look forward to more of them in the future.

February 2019 in Kaohsiung

# 【推薦序】

綠蒂

　　中國的現代詩已有百年歷史，其中亦有不少佳作出現。我曾為了讓中國現代詩推廣到世界各地，讓世界文壇發現中國詩歌的美好，努力提倡中詩英譯或譯成他國文字，但發現詩是困難翻譯的，翻譯等於把詩作以第二種風貌呈現，文字表面意義有外文造詣者均能翻譯，但作品的意境或言外之意是難得在翻譯中呈現，也因為翻譯不出原作的文字節奏，而流於散文形式。本書作者自己創作雙語詩，可表現作品的文字美學並保存創作的意境。

　　羅拔先生詩作，短小精悍，並非常長篇大論，卻言之有物，自己掌握外文能力，不管先有中文詩或英文詩，都能輕鬆駕馭，沒有翻譯障礙，這是本詩集特色。

　　詩歌創道路漫長，有熱情投入者，始能持續不斷向前，盼羅拔先生更上一層樓，俯視詩歌的廣袤大地。

# 【自序】

羅拔

一位詩友說：「若你能同時掌握兩種語言又能寫詩，何不試著寫寫雙語詩呢？」就此開啟了我中英文雙語詩的旅程。

創作雙語詩的過程很有趣，相較於單純的譯詩有很人的不同；譯詩往往是翻譯他人的作品，但雙語詩是自己生下的雙胞胎，身上流著與自己相同的血，面貌相似，各自獨立卻又互補，彷彿生命共同體一般存在著。

後來，很幸運地有些雙語詩登上了詩刊，更開心的是有些作品朋友或詩友看過之後有所感觸，且與我分享。

本雙語詩集分兩輯，輯一的作品是英文在前而中文在後，輯二反之。會如此分別是按照誕生的順序，畢竟雙胞胎也有先出生與後出生的分別，如此以示公平。

能夠寫詩本身就是一件幸運的事情，希望可以幸運一輩子。

二〇一八・十二・三十一　於新北

# 【Prologue】

Rob Chen

A poet once told me, "If you can write in two different languages, why don't you try to write bilingual poems?" And so I started my journey on bilingual poetry.

Writing bilingual poems is rather interesting. Different from translating poetry, it is like giving birth to twins. These twins are apparently alike yet actually different. Most importantly, they are complementary to each other.

I have been fortunate to have some of my bilingual poems published in poetry magazines. I am glad that some of my friends like my works and share their thoughts with me after reading them. It is a great encouragement.

This poetry collection is mainly divided into two parts. In part 1, the English version is put before the Chinese version in pairs. In part 2, it is the opposite. The order depends on the language of which the first poems were written in. I think it's fair to put them in order as they were written.

I think of myself as a lucky guy for I can write poetry. I hope I can write for my whole life.

31st December 2018 in New Taipei City

# 目次

—— 輯二・無夢天堂
Part 2: Heaven Without Dream

詩眠集──羅拔雙語詩集

# Part 1:
## Land Without Sleep

# 輯一‧
## 無眠大地

# Who Steals My Sleep?

A rest is too short to take

A night is too long to stay

Could we be honest

To define a sleep as an escape

And we have stocked daily anxieties

To scare away dreams

So I call myself a thief stealing my sleep

# 誰偷走我的睡眠？

休憩總嫌短
黑夜卻漫長
能不能誠實一些
論定睡眠為逃避
但我們終日囤積焦慮
把夢通通嚇跑
故我自詡為偷眠的賊

# A Personal Statement

A poet writes for love
A love he can not take on
So he writes on
And his life goes on
Until this love is gone

So you might easily find out
A good poem about love
Is too ideal to be real
And it becomes a classic
And a little bit tragic
For you can neither touch nor taste

# 個人論點

詩人為愛而寫
一種他無法承受的愛
於是他寫啊寫
他的生命走啊走
直到此愛消逝

因此你或能輕易發現
一首關於愛的好詩
過度理想而不真實
於是它變成經典
於是有一點感傷
因你摸不著，也嚐不到

# Crows

A thousand dark refugees

Howling, crushing the setting sun

# 鴉

千百個黝黑難民
悲嚎著輾過夕陽

# The Murder Ballad

Today I found my poetry pretty dangerous

They spoke too much and I was furious

I killed them one by one

And dumped their corpses in a trash can

After which I went to wash my hands

I took a look in the mirror, stunned

For all my facial features gone

# 殺戮歌謠

今天發現自己的詩十分凶險
他們說得太多讓我大發雷霆
我一一幹掉他們
屍體倒進垃圾桶
清理完後洗洗手
照鏡子，嚇傻了
我的五官哪去了

# Sashimi

I don't want to be a fish
sliced in dishes,
sent to everybody.
I am not me, not complete.
Like Monday morning,
torn apart by every mouth,
ordered by every phone.
I'm worn out, my boss.

I must be delicious, my boss.
Mustard and soy sauce, no need.
You say that I can be everything.
Your eyes, sushi knives.
Don't push me, I'm dead.
I'm already in your belly.

# 生魚片

我不想當魚
被切進盤子裡
分送給每個人
這不是我，不完整
好似週一早晨
被每一張嘴撕裂
被每一通電話預訂
我累翻了，老闆

我鐵定很可口，老闆
芥末、醬油都不必
你說我是一切
你的一雙眼，兩把壽司刀
別逼我，我死了
已在你肚子裡

# Street Cats

We stop and stare at each other

I meow, she meows back

She meows, I meow back

I meow, she meows back

Silence

We pass by each other

# 野貓

我們停步相視
我喵，她喵
她喵，我喵
我喵，她喵
安靜了
我們錯身而過

# Vow

They cut down other's wings.

Here comes the flood.

They hold each other tight, and pray.

# 誓

他們砍下對方的翅膀
洪水襲來
他們依偎著，禱告

# The White Wine

Under the transparent light

I liquefy

With scent of our fermenting years

And flow

In a nameless street

As a broken bottle of white wine

# 白酒

透明燈光下
我液化
散發著我們發酵歲月的香氣
流竄在
沒有名字的街道
似一瓶碎了的白酒

# Stars

All the night
All our eyes shine
On the sky named website

# 星辰

整個夜晚
我們的雙眼閃爍
在名為網頁的天空

# Salmon: The Migration

Forging ahead in your rapidly shifting moods,

I strive for a conversation, but die,

And become one of your nameless water ghosts.

# 鮭魚：遷徙

在妳流轉的情緒中逆流而上
我渴求對話，卻力竭身亡
成為妳無名水鬼的一員

# The Wall

Watch me, read me, trace me
Write me something, anything
(Now I feel safe)
You are free to shout and cry
(And I feel safer)
Before leaving, could you please
Click on "Like"?

# 牆

看我，讀我，追蹤我
寫些東西給我，隨便都好
（現在我感到安全）
你可以恣意哭叫
（我更加覺得安全）
在你離開之前，可否拜託
點個讚？

# Sister Leaving Home

From the very beginning, the oldest time
Childhood engraved on garden trees
Fish in the pool, kittens sleeping at the door
Remember these, for you are leaving home

Rooms with games, hide and seeks,
Dolls on pillows and beds,
Yellow duck in the bathtub, long time ago
With scent of the alley by the street
Where we had been running and playing
Remember these, for you are leaving home

We must leave home for old men's freedom
Like they watched us skating down from the slope
We are not little, they are not strong
Remember these, for you are leaving home

# 小妹離家

在最早最老的時光
花園的樹上刻著童年
魚優游池中，貓酣睡門前
勿忘此景，在妳離家之前

裝滿遊戲、捉迷藏的房間
玩偶四散在枕頭與床上
浴缸裡的黃色小鴨，好久以前
街旁的小巷飄著芬芳
我倆曾在此追逐嬉戲
勿忘此景，在妳離家之前

我們必須離家，把自由交還老人
像當年他們守望著從斜坡頂溜下的我們
妳我不再幼弱，他倆不再強壯
勿忘此景，在妳離家之前

# Gradually

I see you withering by days

Smiles remain, messages engraved

I know you

I don't know you

I am still decoding

Words you've spoken

My heart is broken

For you are becoming shadows

With unfamiliar names

# 漸

看你們日漸凋零
笑容依舊，卻畫著訊息
我認得你們
我是否還認得你們
我還在解析
你們的話語
心都碎了
你們成了影子
與陌生的名字

# Dream #10

After falling down many times in tears

She becomes a fish, swimming out of her lover's eyes

# 夢境之十

一次次跌坐在淚水之中
她變成一尾魚，從愛人的眼裡游出

# Something/Anything

After work they ate together, read together,
and listened to rock and roll together.
When they had time, they watched a movie
and slept in each other's arms, dreaming
through the cracks of reality.

# 某些事，任何事

下班後他們一起吃飯，一起看書
一起聽搖滾歌曲
若還有時間，看部電影
再睡在彼此的臂彎間，夢
在現實的縫隙中

# Ann

I won't go far

For we've been through war

Ann, with dinner delicious

Your smiles are tender

I have no more request

But a life like this forever

# 安

我不會走遠
戰爭早已過去
安，晚餐真好
妳笑得溫柔
我別無他求
惟如此生活

# The Abattoir

Fat, thin, old, little, plump and young

Sheep, being transported

By the tongue of a department store

To heaven

# 屠宰場

胖的、瘦的、老的、小的、青春豐滿的
羊兒們，搭著百貨公司的舌頭
上天堂

# Losing Weights

When anger becomes poems

When joy becomes poems

When sadness becomes poems

I stay in shape

# 減肥

當憤怒變成詩
當喜悅變成詩
當悲傷變成詩
我保持好身材

# Cake

You yummy victim
Bitten by air condition
Softly sit, lazily lean
For a calm life
But dream
Windows to be broken
For a wild flight

# 蛋糕

你這可口的獵物
讓冷氣一口口咬著
軟趴趴坐著，懶洋洋靠著
平靜地活著
卻夢見
窗戶猛被擊碎
而你狂野起飛

# Hint

You said cute

He said cute

You meant the kid

But he meant you

# 暗示

妳說可愛
他說可愛
妳說那孩子
但他是說妳

# Cooking

Knives, boiling water
And two shaking hands
I am now in Hell, but
Don't know how to kill
And see, all the sexless
Potatoes, onions and carrots
With uneven scars, yelling
To be punished equally
Like all men and women
Who are in fact no less guilty

# 下廚

刀具、滾水
與一雙發抖的手
我置身地獄，卻
不知如何行刑
看見，雌雄難辨的
馬鈴薯、洋蔥、蘿蔔
滿身凹凸不一的刀疤，齊聲大喊
賞罰必得公平
世上男男女女
罪孽豈比我輕

# The Small House

In the small house lived a family
They killed invaders who came in
They killed relatives who came out
They had their own theories

Some police knocked on the door
Some passengers looked in
They shouted, chased them out

How did they earn their living?
They grew food in the backyard
Local and sweet
But the weather wasn't sweet
And the day came

They were starving and eating their family
Day by day, the house was screaming
And empty in the end
The house fell apart, and their bones were exposed
White and pure, like their souls

# 小屋

小屋裡住著一家人
他們殺死進來的外人
他們殺死出去的親人
他們有自己的理論

警察敲門
路人投目
他們咆哮，趕走他們

他們怎麼活？
在後院種植食物
土生土長，滋味甜美
但天氣可不甜美
於是那天來到

他們因為飢餓而吃自己的家人
一天又一天，屋子不斷尖叫
終歸空寂
傾頹時，大家看見他們的骨骸
純白如雪，一如他們的靈魂

# A Drunk Ballad

Our love will be extinct like the dodo

Too slow, too heavy, and too gentle

To survive in the concrete jungle

So give me a kiss, and another

And we can let go in ease

Since no other could reproduce

A song like this, we shall be glad

And sell it to the world

Yet we will be damned, and blamed

Purity is a crime mocking all rules

So give me your hand, let us jump

Into a rocket, to the outer space

To teach life on Mars to love

# 醉之謠

我們的愛必像渡渡鳥般絕種

太慢、太重、太柔

不能在鋼筋叢林中存活

吻我一下吧，再一下

你我就可以放手

若無人能夠複製

這樣的歌曲，我們該開心

並將它賣給世界

但我們必定被詛咒與譴責

過度純粹是嘲諷世界的罪

來，把手給我，跳進

火箭之中，飛向太空

去教火星上的生物如何去愛

# The Gambler

The gambler gambles for an ideal future
The price is paid by the other family members
He has his own theories, speaking out loud
Against the voice of the others, whose anger inside

The gambler refuses to compromise
With his wife and daughter's tears
And he blocks the news, let no relatives know
He insists he is right, telling lies
That he will win, and the family will rise

The gambler's wife keeps suffering
The gambler's daughter stop tolerating
The gambler's son starts to fight
The gambler cannot take money from his family anymore
They reject to support his radical thought, and realize
He's a man with selfish goals, but regards himself as majority
The gambler begs and begs, but gets nothing at all

The gambler carries enormous debt home

He hides himself in the closet

Lenders come, and yell to pull him out

At one night his family kicks him out

He weeps and walks, and his shadow fades out


The family retrieves their normal pace

They start running business and their reputation rises

Their bank accounts finally have something after 24 years

But the gambler father is always in their mind

Like a ghost misty and light, mumbling the past

# 賭徒

賭徒賭一個理想的未來
代價讓家人付
他有自己的論調，大言不慚
壓過其他人的聲音，他們怒火中燒

賭徒拒絕屈服於妻女的淚水
他封鎖消息，不讓親戚知曉
堅持己見，謊稱
他會贏，家族將旺

賭徒的太太繼續受苦
賭徒的女兒不再忍耐
賭徒的兒子開始還擊
賭徒再也無法從家人手裡拿錢
他們拒絕支持他荒謬的想法，知道
他只為了個人目標，自認眾人代表
賭徒乞求再乞求，還是甚麼都拿不到

賭徒背了數不清的債回家
他把自己藏在衣櫃裡
債主來了，吼說要拖他出去
在一個夜裡他的家人把他踢出去
他流著眼淚走開，身影淡去

他的家人重拾正常的步調
開始做生意，家族興旺
二十四年後，他們的帳戶不再是空的
但賭徒父親依然長存他們心中
像是迷濛又輕佻的幽魂，咕噥著過去

# Parting

On the bus there's only silence
Unlike before, as we were
Talking and laughing, sometimes
Blamed by sleepy passengers
So short the time and our way home
30 minutes, how small it is to a day
But so happy I was, I guess you too
Secrets we shared, jokes we told
Were taken away when you left
Like the other passengers, always
I sink into a full blank called
SLEEP

# 離

巴士上只有寂靜
不同以往，我們
有說有笑，幾次
被疲倦的乘客責備
歸返之路途短暫
半小時，在一天之中多麼渺小
卻很開心，猜妳也是
分享的八卦，說過的笑話
都隨妳離去
我已像其他乘客一樣，總是
沉入完全的空白，名為
睡

# Twins

I spoke to myself
Myself never replied

I broke the mirror in anger
But he hid in my shadow
And I ran into darkness
But he swam into my blood

I no more spoke to myself
And he cried, but it was I
Flooded by tears

# 雙生

我對自己說話
自己不曾回應

我憤怒地打碎鏡子
但他躲進我影子裡
我衝向黑暗找尋
他卻游進我血液

我不再對自己說話
他哭了，但怎麼是我
被淚淹沒

# A New Year's Song

A year passed like a morning piss

You don't want to face it

And you won't miss it

But you must do it

So just get up, let the rain drop

And make a wish to Niagara Falls

# 新年之歌

一年如晨尿流逝
不想面對
也不會懷念
終得執行一次
起床了，讓雨落下
朝尼加拉瓜瀑布許個願吧

# Garbage Bag

Try to put on a suitable clothing

Better a single color, to cover my colorful emotions

And twice a week, throw myself away

# 垃圾袋

幫自己套件合身衣物
最好素色，蓋住鮮豔情緒
每週兩次，準時丟掉自己

# Zen

You ask me why I write

I say I must be tired of

Carrying all the toxic daydreams

So I let them go, and watch them climb in black

They grow wild, but I survive

# 禪說

你問我為何寫作
我說是厭倦了
終日肩負著劇毒的白日夢
我放了它們，看著它們黑溜溜地爬行
它們日漸猖狂，我卻得以倖存

# The Fictional Lover

She didn't often message me

She didn't even put eyes on me

But she, to my surprise,

Secretly read my poems

# 雲端情人

她不常丟我訊息
甚至不瞧我一眼
但我很驚訝，她
祕密地讀我的詩

# Gone

They're all gone

Leaving you pondering

About the beginning

And wondering

Is it only you with fists tight

For a fight, without knowing why?

# 逝

都走了
留下你獨自思索
源頭
疑惑
是否只有自己緊握拳頭
爭鬥，卻不知何故？

# The Copyist

You don't know
I am depicting you
Like the squirrel by my window
Caught in my mobile phone

Don't worry
If you go, just go
Imagination will fill
The remaining parts of you

But is that you?
It's alright
When I write
I am not me either

# 臨摹者

妳不知道
我在臨摹妳
像窗外的松鼠
被我用手機捕捉

別擔心
妳想走，就走
想像力會填滿
尚未完成的部分

但那真是妳？
沒關係
當我提筆
我亦非我

# Amour

When you are tired I will sing you a song

A song that calls our youth

A song that we both know

A song that remains...not the same, but fresh

As the sunrise everyday

And we will sing it until a dove takes it over

So you won't feel that life is long

# 愛慕

當妳累了我會替妳唱首歌
一首讓我們憶起青春的歌
一首我們都不陌生
卻不盡相同，有著新鮮感
彷彿日出之歌
我們一起唱，待白鴿將它啣去
妳便不會覺得生命太漫長

# The Whistling Kettle

I waited for the boiling water,
And Daddy called me in.

He showed me his toy.
I didn't like the toy.
He didn't like my shirt.
He didn't like my skirt.
He ordered me to hold his toy.
I said no and he was mad.
He punished me with the toy.
The water was crying.
He told me to get out.
He said he needed a rest.

I waited for the boiling water,
And Daddy dragged me in.

# 鳴笛水壺

我看著燒開水，爸爸
叫我進去

他拿出他的玩具
我不喜歡他的玩具
他不喜歡我的衣服
他不喜歡我的裙子
他要我拿著他的玩具
我說不要他很生氣
他用玩具懲罰我
水嗚嗚的哭了
他叫我滾出去
他說他要休息

我看著燒開水，爸爸
拽我進去

# My Babe Monster

## ——To Thesis

I was a child unfamiliar to life,

Married with my blind passion.

I was pregnant with you,

My invisible babe.

You had been sleeping all day

And growing up silently in my brain.

You were a gluttonous baby

Draining my train of thought

And my happiness and hopes

As your essential nutrition.

I got a migraine afterwards

And fell ill with no fixed schedule.


My heart broke each time I thought of you,

My dearest baby.

When my youth was wandering on the pages,

My dream could never escape from the hard covers.

How dazzling I was when I kept vomiting

In the labyrinth of words.

You were doomed to be malnourished, a fateful freak.

My babe monster,

I gave birth to you under my fingertips.

You, so unsightly, but do not worry.

I would apply cosmetics on you every day and night,

Until the venerable professors hold you in their arms.

Yet I had to hold a public hearing for you,

And disguised you as a hopeful child in advance.

I would shout myself blue in the face,

Until the stern judges throw an unwilling smile to you.

# 我的妖怪娃娃

——致論文

我是不諳世事的孩子
與盲目的熱情交歡，懷了你
我的隱形娃娃
你日日夜夜沉睡
在我的腦裡悄悄長大
你是貪心的寶寶
吸取我的思緒
榨乾我的快樂希望
作為你必須的營養
我因此罹患偏頭痛
不定期地發作

想起你就斷腸
我親愛的寶寶
當青春漂泊紙上
夢卻走不出扉頁
我暈眩在書的迷宮，不斷嘔出文字
你的養分不足，注定殘缺

我的妖怪娃娃

我自指尖產下你

醜陋如你，也毋須煩惱

我會日日夜夜幫你化妝

直到德高望重的師長將你懷抱

而我仍需為你辦一場聽證會

將你偽裝成前途似錦的孩子

在神色肅穆的法官前，替你聲嘶力竭的辯駁

直到他們對你擠出一絲勉強的笑

# The Siren

I

Your silence
cuts me deeper
than your song.

II

Your smiles grow
into endless lavender fields.
Like a wild child,
I get lost, but miss not home.

## III

Drowned in your whirpool alike
laughter, whispers and silence,
even when I'm home.

## IV

Cease singing.
Nothing is left between us
but illusions.

V

I listen to the rain—
simply beautiful, and true.
And wonder why I had been sunken
in her artful melodies.

## Afterword

I listened to wild songs.
I listen to mild rains.
And I will listen to
Nothingness.

# 海妖

一

妳的沉默
劃傷我，更甚
妳的歌

二

妳的微笑蔓延
成為無垠薰衣草田
好似個野孩子
我迷了路，卻不想家

三

溺斃在妳漩渦般的
笑靨、低語與沉默裡
縱然我已歸鄉

四

停止歌唱吧
我們之間已無所膌
僅存幻覺

## 五

我聽著雨
簡單優美，且真
疑惑著為何曾深陷
她那狡獪的旋律

## 後話

我曾聽狂野的歌
我聽著溫和的雨
而我即將聆聽
虛無

# Now That We Shall Part

I am always too shy to say goodbye

But you must know I care about you, all the time

Like watching a film, I stay until the credits close

Nothing is trivial, nothing should be skipped

For we are all made of details

Like back-and-forth messages, emotional

All moments are written, but some you may have forgotten

Alright, I'll leave curtains drawn

Love, hate and doubt, let the sun speak

For I am too shy to say goodbye

# 別離此刻

我總是羞於道別
但請你明瞭，我無時不關切著你
像欣賞一部電影，總待到字幕跑完
沒什麼是次要，沒什麼該被漏掉
我們都由細節構成
彷彿來來往往的情緒信息
書寫了每一刻，或許部分你已忘記
不要緊，我會將簾幕拉起
愛、恨與疑慮，就讓太陽說去
因我仍羞於道別

# Mimicry

I could always fit in
the shape of your voice
unconsciously.

I am getting stronger.
Yet you still consider me
as an invader.

The door is neither open
nor closed. So
let my island be yours.

# 擬態

總能迎合
你的聲形
卻不自覺

變得堅強
仍被視為
入侵的人

門沒開
也沒關，那
就讓我的島嶼歸屬於你

註：「也沒關，那」原作「也沒開，那」於2019.10月再版更正

# 輯二・
## 無夢天堂

# Part 2:
# Heaven Without Dream

# 悅讀

在字裡行間聽見妳的心跳
一種纖細
雍容自然的旋律
彷彿我這一生

我看著妳
妳看著我
我僅翻閱了幾頁
妳卻把我讀透
說出我唇間醞釀的字句
看穿我心底掩藏的話語
妳是誰？

妳是誰？
如此輕易地讓我棄械
我還有工作要忙，家人要養
那
那我們一起私奔好不好？

# Reading

Hear your heartbeat through words in lines—
Melody of delicacy,
Gentleness and dignity,
Epitomizing my whole life.

Stare at you,
And stared by you.
Few pages I turn.
Yet you read me through.
Foretell the words brewing between my lips,
Foresee the language hidden secretly in my mind
Who are you?

Who are you?
You disarm me easily.
I have a family to feed, and works to do.
So
May we elope?

# 煙

吐出濃嗆的三十年

鬆手

蒂落

孤獨燒

# Smoke

Puff the pungent thirty years

Release the hand

The cigarette butt falls

Solitude burns

# 甜食怪

我含著巧克力
時間含著我
溶解

# Dessert Monster

I hold a chocolate in my mouth
Time holds me in hers
Dissolving

# 暈

誰把往事吐了一地
在空蕩無人的月台？
甸甸的公事包下
我也彎腰　作嘔

# Faint

Who threw up all the past
On the platform with nobody else?
Under my heavy briefcase
I am bending over, vomiting

# 詩奴

他請我寫
她要我寫
它叫我寫
我逼我自己寫

太陽不耐煩地跳進海裡泡澡
換好奇的月亮爬上窗
看笑話

# Slave of Poetry

He tells me to write
She wants me to write
It asks me to write
I push myself to write

The impatient sun jumps to the sea for a bath
The curious moon climbs on my window
Laughing at me

# 潛行者

他聽妳聽的歌曲
他看妳看的電影
他的眼睛　他的耳朵
仍在妳牆上　爬
妳在牆後　看準按鈕
手指朝下　封殺

# The Stalker

He listens to songs you listened

He watches movies you watched

His eyes and ears

Climbing on your wall

You behind the wall, looking at the button

One finger down, BLOCK

# 雙弦

若我們都是說書人
彈奏往日琴弦
一條名之母
一條名之父

---

註：致電影《酷寶：魔弦詛咒》，動畫中的傑作

# Two Strings

If we are all storytellers

Plucking at the strings of past

One we call it mother

The other we call it father

---

Note: Dedicated to *Kubo and the Two Strings*, a masterpiece of animation

# 終曲

我不前進了
要不　墜落的時候
還得看你在懸崖上攤手
問：誰的錯？

# The End

I am not approaching anymore.
Otherwise, while falling
I will watch you shrugging shoulders on the cliff,
Asking, "Whose fault?"

## 《預言者保羅之書》
### ——獻給章魚哥保羅與2010世足

### 天才的寂寞

嗑完第八本考前猜題後

他再也撐不下了

碰　一頭栽上書　開始打呼

一群同學搖醒他

人手一張他滿分的罪狀

雙眼噴火

說：「這次我們真要煮了你！」

## 世界的殘酷

他的眼睛衝太遠

身軀落後　被

那群心碎的賭徒追殺

他們手持鍋鏟　憤怒地說：

「吃了他！吃了他！

吃了他（的力量）！」

眼睛向鎂光燈尋求政治庇護

逃進網路　鑽進報紙

在謾罵與掌聲中　看見

歲月狠狠攔下漸漸無力的身軀

## 先知的離去

祂開口

他們下注

他們收錢

他們囚禁祂

他們餵祂

他們替祂拍照

祂不再開口

他越來越老

牠閉上眼睛

它的一生被圈在照片上

# Book for Paul the Prophet

——Dedicated to Paul the Octopus and World Cup 2010

Loneliness of a Genius

After swallowing eight test preparation books,

Paul was totally full.

His head knocked on his desk,

And began snoring.

His classmates woke him up.

Each handed a copy of Paul's perfect-scored test papers

With eyes on fire,

And madly they said, "We're gonna cook you this time."

## Cruelty of the World

His eyes ran too fast,

Leaving his body far behind.

A group of heartbroken gamblers were chasing his body

With spatulas on their hands,

And shouting, "Eat him! Eat him!

Eat (his power of prediction)!"

His eyes begged cameras for a political asylum,

And ran into the internet and newspapers for safety.

Besieged by both applause and abuse, his eye saw

Time was stopping his powerless body from escaping.

## Departure of the Prophet

He spoke.

They staked.

They collected money.

They imprisoned him.

They fed him.

They took photos of him.

His mouth closed.

He was getting old.

His eyes closed.

His whole life was circled in photographs.

# 紅流
## ——悼辭世的祖父母

他倆僅是輕輕告別了陽台
如蜻蜓　點向記憶的湖泊
圈出漩渦

她藉目擊者電話裡顫抖的聲音道別
我啞然地摸索她墜落時的表情
墜落後的姿態
失去恐懼或哭的能力
他憑著頑強的信念　延長自己的生命線
握過槍　握過勳章
黃埔軍校十三期畢業的上校
多次在炮火中制止死神咆哮　微笑著回家
卻終跟著她的步伐
猝
然
降
落
碎成一地的鰥守孤獨
　（是夜天邊高掛的鐮刀是死神勝利的旗幟）

薛西弗斯推著石頭　石頭自山頂滾落
薛西弗斯推著石頭　石頭自山頂滾落
兩條河緩緩流過我的夢
交會處　一磐石佇立著
緘默著　懺悔著　點滴著
紅色的淚

# The Red Flood
## ——In memory of my departed grandparents

They just departed gently from the balcony,

as dragonflies skimmed the sea of memory,

circling a whirlpool.


She bid us farewell through the shivering voice of a stranger.

I dumbly depicted her look when falling,

her appearance after the fall,

and lost my ability to cry and fear.

By a tenacious faith he had prolonged his lifeline.

Medals and guns in hands,

a colonel he was,

from the 13th session graduate of Whampoa Military Academy.

For so many times he prevented the Death from roaring,

and smiled home.

But in the end he followed her way

F
A
L
L
I
N
G

into pieces of a widower's loneliness.

(A reaping-hook hanging high in the sky

as a flag of victory from the Death)


Sisyphus pushed the rock atop, and the rock rolled down.

Sisyphus pushed the rock atop, and the rock rolled down.

Two streams slowly flew across my dream.

At its confluence, a rock stood

in silence, repenting and dripping

tears in red.

# 中年

起霧了
但你清楚
直走

# Middle Age

The mist is rising

But you are clear

And going straight

# 花

從螢幕上
摘幾朵妳的話
壓在枕頭下
作夢

# Flowers

From the screen

I pluck petals of your words

And tuck them under my pillow

To dream

# 捉迷藏

可以禮貌
也可以裝沒看到

可以風趣
也可以語帶惡意

隔著螢幕
沒一張臉是清楚的

誰有情緒
誰就當鬼

# Seek and Hide

You can be polite
Or you can be blind

You can be humorous
Or you can be vicious

Behind screens
No face is clear

Those with emotion exposed
Are the ghosts

# 夜襲

那一身黑的女刺客
悄悄迷昏我的同伴
我一抬頭
竟已被她黑袍所囚
她究竟圖些甚麼？
我把手裡的黑咖啡握得更緊

# The Night Attack

The female assassin in black

Quietly made my compenions in coma.

I lifted up my head

And found myself caged under a black robe.

What did she really want?

I held my black coffee in hands even tighter.

# 除濕機

嘮叨一整個下午
戛然沉默
我苦水滿腹的中年

# Dehumidifier

Murmuring for the whole afternoon

Suddenly speechless

My middle age with bitter water in stomach

# 標點

想像
妳的笑畫下我今日的句號

# The Punctuation

Imagining

Your smile draws the full stop of today

# 重逢

這次我
拾起散落我倆腳邊的音符
譜一首詩，給妳

# The Reunion

This time, I

Picked up notes by our feet

And composed a poem, for you

# 浪漫

似不斷轉動的車輪
絞我思緒
我把現實吐了一床

# Romantic

Like a non-stop spinning wheel

Twisting my thoughts

I puked up reality all over my bed

# 突變

把恐懼壓進夢中
養一池魚
牠們的牙越長越利
醒來後，穿上西裝
開門，一陣昏
從腦門
倏地穿出千百根刺

# Transformation

Press down fear into a dream

To feed a pool of fish

Their tooth are getting sharper

Put suits on while awake

Open the door, feel dizzy

From the forehead

A thousand thorns are dashing out

# 孩子

可是他坐在一棵楓樹上
不知道已是秋天

總是嗚咽
以滿是紅色條紋的手背
拭淚
什麼是家？
怒吼酒瓶玻璃瘀青
空氣裡　迴盪著　他
不敢直視的魔鬼
不願聆聽的咒語

所以他仍坐在那楓樹上
不知道已是春天

# The Child

Yet he sits in a maple tree,
Unaware of the coming Fall.

Always weeping, he wipes his tears
With the back of his hand
On which red stripes overspread.
What is home to him?
Winebottlesbrokenglassbruisesscreams.
In the air, a demon is whirling,
Whom he dares not look into the face,
And chanting dreadful incantations.

So he still sits in the maple tree,
Unaware of the coming Spring.

# 臉

他從沒看過媽媽
聽說是很久很久以前的事了
醉酒的男人　荒唐的散彈
媽媽美麗的青春急診　無效

夢裡媽媽總戴著眼罩　抱著他
有一次媽媽說要拿下眼罩
他說不要不要
他知道媽媽很愛他　他知道

後記：
新聞─美國奧立岡州廿七歲婦人克莉茜·史泰茲十一年前遭霰彈槍誤
擊臉部而毀容，也喪失視力，但她仍勇敢生活下去並嫁人生子，唯一
缺憾是只能戴眼罩面對自己的幼兒。如今專家為她精心製作一張「義
臉」（prosthetic face），她在動手術戴上後，終於能夠以接近天生的
容貌，讓孩子看到媽媽的臉。見中時電子報（2010/07/18）

# Face

He has never seen his mother.

It was long long time ago-

A drunken man, and his absurd bullets.

Her beautiful youth was sent to ER,

Certified dead.


When dreaming, his mother always held him

With a patch on her face.

One day she wanted to take it off.

But he said no, no.

He knew she loved him, he knew.


Note:
Inspired by the news "Disfigured Gun-shot Survivor Faces Her Young Son For The First Time Thanks To Pio-neering Surgeons' Pros-thetic Mask" in MailOnline World News, 17th July 2018

# 末日

當世界只剩打字的聲音
別生氣
我依然愛妳

# The Day the World Ends

When nothing is left but sounds of typing

Don't get mad

I love you all the same

# 變形記
──致宅男

關上電源
他便僵硬

在床上
蜷成一圈電線

# Metamorphosis

## ——To An Otaku

Power off.
He feels stiff all over.

On the bed,
He's coiling, transforming
Into a rigid electric wire.

# 鳥
——致捐血

銀喙子進

紅喙子出

銀喙子進

紅喙子出


上臂裹著紗布來來去去的耶穌

# Bird

——To Blood Donation

Silver beak in

Red beak out

Silver beak in

Red beak out

Bandages around their arms

One Jesus left and another came

# 怪物的孩子

怪物的孩子被拎起
丟進推車裡
他們扭開它的頭蓋骨
他們戳它的腦
放光它白色的血
他們歡呼勝利　他們讚嘆正義
他們說是天的旨意
不許異議

# The Monster's Child

The monster's child is carried

And thrown into a cart

They twist off its skull

They stab on its brain

They drain off his white blood

They yell for victory

They hail to justice

They say it's God's will

Do not blaspheme

# 【後記】

羅拔

　　該感謝老天賜我失眠的天賦，我的眾多詩作誕生於無眠的夜。當然，更要感謝因此被我打擾的家人，沒有他們的包容，不會有這本詩集的誕生。

　　要怎麼定義一本詩集呢？它就像一個花園，裡面長滿了花花草草。有些你認得，有些我認得，也有些我們都認得或不認得。認得的，即是屬於你我的私人訊息，有些長得奇形怪狀，有的看起來不甚道德，請別介意。畢竟，文字的土壤不會選擇生物，而是被生物選擇。

　　出口到了，謝謝光臨我的詩園。

二〇一九・一・一　於台北

# 【 Epilogue 】

Rob Chen

I must be grateful for my gift of insomnia. If I spent too much time sleeping, many poems would not have been written. And I want to thank my family members who have been bothered by my writing habit. Without their tolerance, this poetry collection would not have been born.

To me, a poetry collection is like a garden with plants. Some plants you recognize and some you do not. You may take the former as personal messages for you. Some of my poems may look strange and immoral. It is alright. The soil of words does not choose lives, but is chosen by lives.

This is the exit. Thank you for visiting my poetry garden.

1st January 2019 in Taipei City

語言文學類　PG2249　吹鼓吹詩人叢書41

# 詩眠集
## ──羅拔雙語詩集

作　　者／羅　拔
主　　編／蘇紹連
責任編輯／陳慈蓉
圖文排版／楊家齊
封面設計／楊廣榕

發 行 人／宋政坤
法律顧問／毛國樑　律師
出版發行／秀威資訊科技股份有限公司
　　　　　114台北市內湖區瑞光路76巷65號1樓
　　　　　電話：+886-2-2796-3638　傳真：+886-2-2796-1377
　　　　　http://www.showwe.com.tw
劃撥帳號／19563868　戶名：秀威資訊科技股份有限公司
　　　　　讀者服務信箱：service@showwe.com.tw
展售門市／國家書店（松江門市）
　　　　　104台北市中山區松江路209號1樓
　　　　　電話：+886-2-2518-0207　傳真：+886-2-2518-0778
網路訂購／秀威網路書店：https://store.showwe.tw
　　　　　國家網路書店：https://www.govbooks.com.tw

2019年10月　BOD二刷
定價：250元
版權所有　翻印必究
本書如有缺頁、破損或裝訂錯誤，請寄回更換

國家圖書館出版品預行編目

詩眠集：羅拔雙語詩集 / 羅拔著. -- 一版. -- 臺北市：
　　秀威資訊科技, 2019.04
　　　　面；　　公分. -- (語言文學類；PG2249)(吹鼓吹
詩人叢書；41)
　　BOD版
　　ISBN 978-986-326-670-9(平裝)


851.486　　　　　　　　　　　　　　108002575

# 讀者回函卡

感謝您購買本書，為提升服務品質，請填妥以下資料，將讀者回函卡直接寄回或傳真本公司，收到您的寶貴意見後，我們會收藏記錄及檢討，謝謝！
如您需要了解本公司最新出版書目、購書優惠或企劃活動，歡迎您上網查詢或下載相關資料：http:// www.showwe.com.tw

您購買的書名：＿＿＿＿＿＿＿＿＿＿＿＿＿＿＿＿＿＿＿＿＿＿＿
出生日期：＿＿＿＿＿年＿＿＿＿＿月＿＿＿＿＿日
學歷：□高中 (含) 以下　　□大專　　□研究所 (含) 以上
職業：□製造業　□金融業　□資訊業　□軍警　□傳播業　□自由業
　　　□服務業　□公務員　□教職　　□學生　□家管　　□其它＿＿＿
購書地點：□網路書店　□實體書店　□書展　□郵購　□贈閱　□其他
您從何得知本書的消息？
　　□網路書店　□實體書店　□網路搜尋　□電子報　□書訊　□雜誌
　　□傳播媒體　□親友推薦　□網站推薦　□部落格　□其他＿＿＿＿＿
您對本書的評價：(請填代號　1.非常滿意　2.滿意　3.尚可　4.再改進)
　　封面設計＿＿＿　版面編排＿＿＿　內容＿＿＿　文／譯筆＿＿＿　價格＿＿＿
讀完書後您覺得：
　　□很有收穫　□有收穫　□收穫不多　□沒收穫


對我們的建議：＿＿＿＿＿＿＿＿＿＿＿＿＿＿＿＿＿＿＿＿＿＿＿

＿＿＿＿＿＿＿＿＿＿＿＿＿＿＿＿＿＿＿＿＿＿＿＿＿＿＿＿＿＿＿＿

＿＿＿＿＿＿＿＿＿＿＿＿＿＿＿＿＿＿＿＿＿＿＿＿＿＿＿＿＿＿＿＿

＿＿＿＿＿＿＿＿＿＿＿＿＿＿＿＿＿＿＿＿＿＿＿＿＿＿＿＿＿＿＿＿

11466
台北市內湖區瑞光路 76 巷 65 號 1 樓

**秀威資訊科技股份有限公司**　　　收

BOD 數位出版事業部

............................................................

（請沿線對折寄回，謝謝！）

姓　　名：＿＿＿＿＿＿＿＿　年齡：＿＿＿＿　性別：□女　□男

郵遞區號：□□□□□

地　　址：＿＿＿＿＿＿＿＿＿＿＿＿＿＿＿＿＿＿＿＿

聯絡電話：(日) ＿＿＿＿＿＿＿＿＿　(夜) ＿＿＿＿＿＿＿＿＿

E-mail：＿＿＿＿＿＿＿＿＿＿＿＿＿＿＿＿＿＿＿＿